Welcome Little Liam !
Enjoy this story
about love.

Hugs + love
Moe

This book belongs to

_____

Mama Loves Me

Anna
Pignataro

Scholastic Canada Ltd.
Toronto New York London Auckland Sydney
Mexico City New Delhi Hong Kong Buenos Aires

Scholastic Canada Ltd.
604 King Street West, Toronto, Ontario M5V 1E1, Canada

Scholastic Inc.
557 Broadway, New York, NY 10012, USA

Scholastic Australia Pty Limited
PO Box 579, Gosford, NSW 2250, Australia

Scholastic New Zealand Limited
Private Bag 94407, Botany, Manukau 2163, New Zealand

Scholastic Children's Books
Euston House, 24 Eversholt Street, London NW1 1DB, UK

www.scholastic.ca

Library and Archives Canada Cataloguing in Publication

Pignataro, Anna, 1965-, author
Mama loves me / Anna Pignataro.
Contents: Mama, will you hold my hand? -- Mama, how long
will you love me? -- Mama, will I be yours forever?

ISBN 978-1-4431-4833-7 (hardback)

I. Title.

PZ7.P614586Ma 2016   j823'.914   C2015-908665-5

Mama, How Long Will You Love Me? text and illustrations copyright © 2006 by Anna Pignataro. First published as *Always* by Scholastic Press, a division of Scholastic Australia Pty Limited in 2006.
Mama, Will You Hold My Hand? text and illustrations copyright © 2009 by Anna Pignataro. First published as *Together* by Scholastic Press, a division of Scholastic Australia Pty Limited in 2009.
Mama, Will I Be Yours Forever? text and illustrations copyright © 2012 by Anna Pignataro. First published as *Forever* by Scholastic Press, a division of Scholastic Australia Pty Limited in 2012.
This edition published by Scholastic Canada Ltd. in 2016.

6 5 4 3 2 1   Printed in Malaysia 108   16 17 18 19 20

Contents

Mama, How Long Will You Love Me? . . . 7

Mama, Will You Hold My Hand?. 37

Mama, Will I Be Yours Forever? 67

Mama,
How Long Will You Love Me?

In a brambly forest, Sammy asked,
"How long will you be my mother?"

"Always," said Mama.

Underneath a big old elm, Sammy asked,
"Mama, how long will you love me?"

"Always," Mama smiled.

"How long is always?" Sammy asked.

"Miles and miles forever," said Mama.

"As high as a giant tree . . .

15

16

As magical as a starry night . . .

As wild as a windy day . . .

As wondrous
as a winter snow . . .

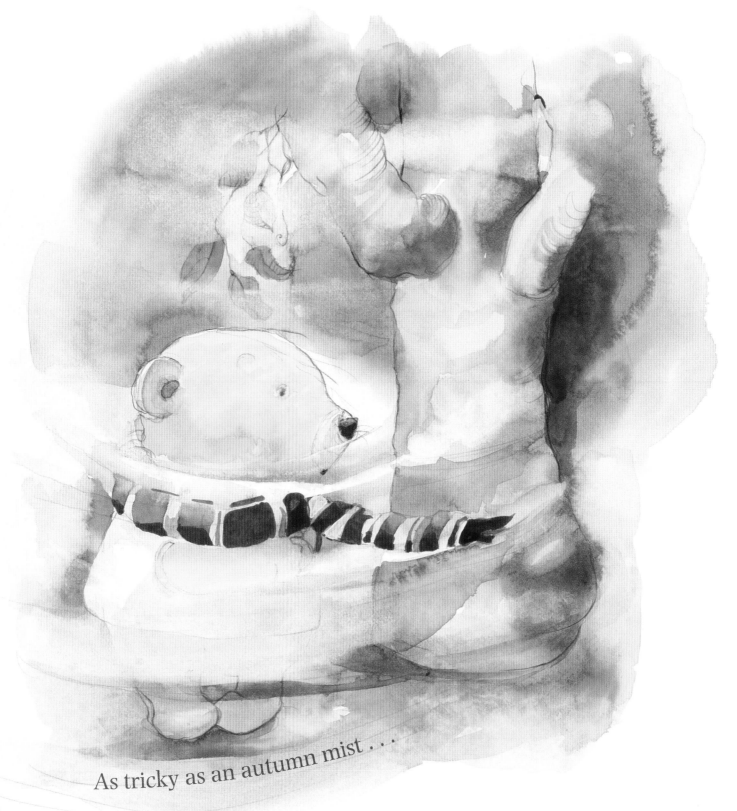

As tricky as an autumn mist . . . .

As soft as a cloudy sky . . .

As **slow** as a sleepy noon . . .

As light as a pink balloon . . .

As
fresh
as
a
summer
shower . . .

As gentle as a
springtime wing . . .

As secret as a birthday wish . . .

As far as the milky moon . . .

As deep as
the deep blue sea . . .

As
quiet
as a
falling
star . . .

As warm as a bedtime snuggle . . .

As sweet as a honey kiss . . .

As precious as
you and me."

"Will there always be you and me?" asked Sammy.

"Miles and miles forever,"
whispered Mama.

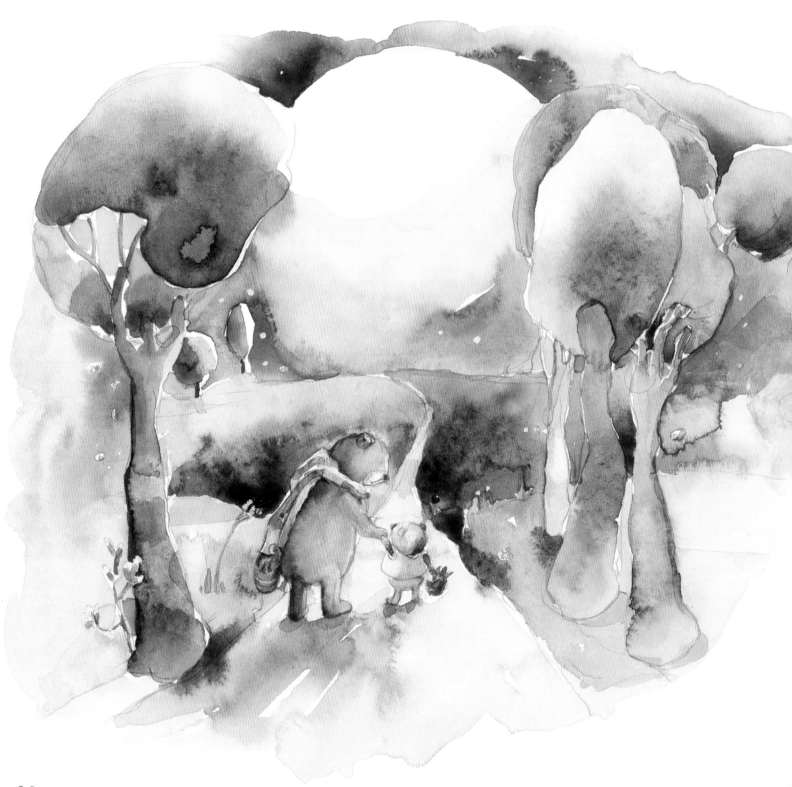

Mama,
Will You Hold My Hand?

As the sun came down behind the
bramble bushes Sammy asked,

"Mama, are you there?"

"I'm right here," said Mama.

Over a rickety bridge Sammy asked,
"Mama, will you hold my hand?"

"I'll hold your hand and you'll hold mine, and we'll go everywhere together," said Mama.

"To the edge of the world?" asked Sammy.

"To the ends of the earth," said Mama.

43

"Over marshy meadows . . .

45

Where the night is still . . .

Into muddy puddles . . .

Out among the treasures . . .

Under swirling skies . . .

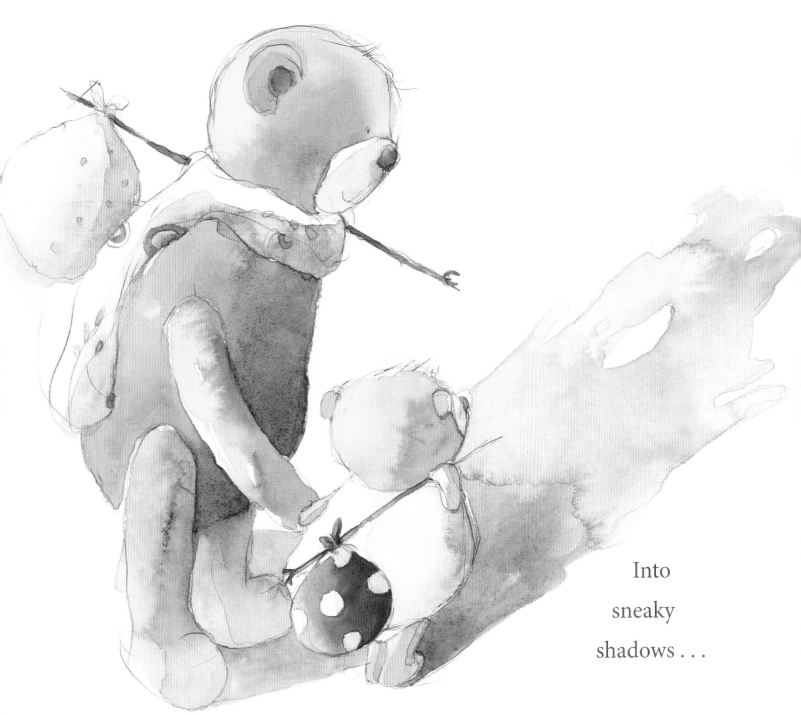

Into
sneaky
shadows . . .

Under ruby feathers . . .

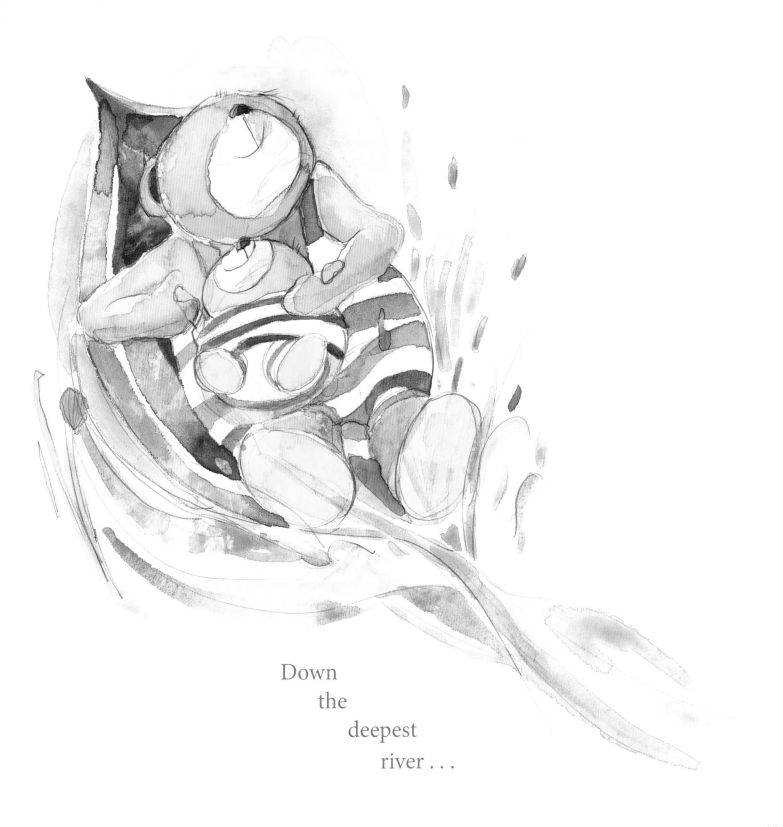

Down
the
deepest
river . . .

Over slippery places . . .

Into wavy waters . . .

To the brightest star . . .

Up the highest mountain . . .

On a rainbow's tail . . .

In your wildest dreams . . .

62

To another world."

"Mama, will we never let go?"
whispered Sammy.

Mama smiled. "We'll always
be together."

Mama,
Will I Be Yours Forever?

Out among the wildflowers rambling
in the meadow, Sammy asked,

"Mama, what is that?"

"It's a cocoon with a tiny caterpillar
inside," said Mama, "until it changes."

69

"Changes?" Sammy asked, lying in the soft grass.

"Soon it will become a beautiful butterfly," said Mama.

"Why, Mama?" asked Sammy.

"There are many
          changes, every day,"
                    said Mama.

73

"A cool morning dawn

becomes a bright sunny day.

Tiny green buds become a field of flowers.

76

A spotty egg hatches

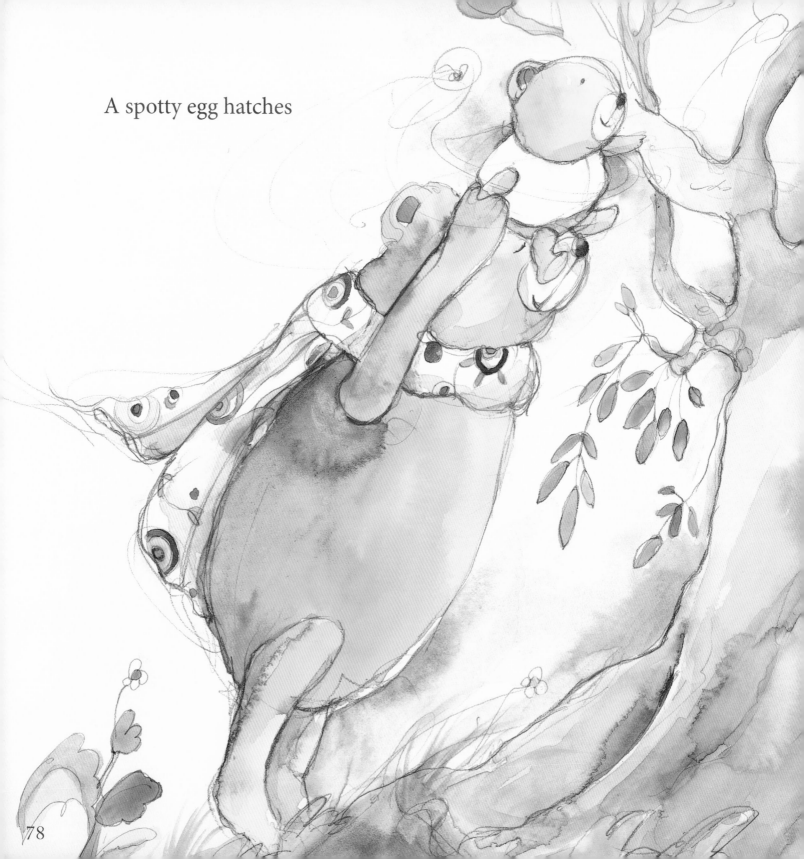

into a baby bird.

A gentle river flows . . .

into seven wild seas . . .

that slowly become little waves lapping at your feet.

A bright yellow day becomes a soft pink dusk.

And a quiet wait . . .

becomes a wonderful surprise."

"Mama, will I change?" asked Sammy.

"You will become big and strong,"
 whispered Mama.

"But you will be my
 little bear forever."